Hugs and Kisses

First published in Switzerland under the title *Mama, ich hab Dich lieb*

No part of this publication may be reproduced in whole or in part, or stored in a retrieval system, or transmitted in any form or by any means, electronic, mechanical, photocopying, recording, or otherwise, without written permission of the publisher. For information regarding permission, write to North-South Books Inc., 1123 Broadway, Suite 800, New York, NY 10010.

ISBN 0-439-38005-7

15 14 13 12 11 10 9   8 9 10 11 / 0

Printed in the U.S.A.

First Scholastic printing, January 2003

Christophe Loupy

Hugs and Kisses

Eve Tharlet

Translated by J. Alison James

SCHOLASTIC INC.
New York Toronto London Auckland Sydney
Mexico City New Delhi Hong Kong Buenos Aires

One morning, Hugs the puppy woke up early.
His mother and father and all his sisters were
still sleeping. Quietly he tiptoed outside. There
was something he had to find out.

"Good morning," called two ducks from the pond.
"What are you doing up so early?"
"I'm finding out something," Hugs said. "Could you please give me a kiss?"
"A kiss?" quacked the ducks. "Of course. Where would you like it?"
"Right here," said Hugs, and he pointed to his cheek.

So the ducks came out of the water and each gave him a kiss: one on the left and one on the right.
Hugs closed his eyes and smiled. He'd never ever had a kiss from a duck!
It was a bit hard of course, and wet, but it was quite refreshing.
Hugs thanked the ducks and went on.

Out in the pasture Hugs saw a horse. "Good morning!"
he called.
"Good morning," answered the horse. "It's nice of you
to visit."
"I was wondering," Hugs said shyly. "Could you please
give me a kiss?"
"A kiss?" neighed the horse.
"Yes, right here." Hugs pointed to his forehead.

So the horse bent down
and gave him a big kiss.
Hugs closed his eyes and
smiled. He'd never ever had
a kiss from a horse!
It was a bit damp of course,
and sticky, but it was
quite warm.
Hugs thanked the horse
and went on.

Soon the puppy found a pig rolling in a puddle of mud.
"Good morning," said Hugs.
"Good morning to you," answered the pig. "What are you
 doing here all alone?"
"I'm finding out something," Hugs said. "Could you please
 give me a kiss?"
"A kiss from me?" grunted the pig.
"Yes, right here." Hugs pointed to the tip of his nose.

So the pig stepped out of the mud and gave him a kiss right on the tip of his nose.

Hugs closed his eyes and smiled. He'd never ever had a kiss from a pig!

It was a bit muddy of course, and the bristles scratched a little, but it was quite tender.

Hugs thanked the pig and went on.

Hugs came to a garden fence. There he spied a rabbit out
among the corn.

"Good morning," he called.

"What are you doing so far from home?" asked the rabbit.

"I'm finding out something," Hugs said. "Could you please
give me a kiss?"

"A kiss from me?" murmured the rabbit.

"Yes, right here." Hugs pointed to his neck.

The rabbit hopped closer and gave him a kiss right in his wrinkled fur.

Hugs closed his eyes and smiled. He'd never ever had a kiss from a rabbit!

It was a bit wiggley of course, and quick, but it was quite soft.

Hugs thanked the rabbit and headed back home.

On the way, Hugs saw a yellow butterfly.

"Good morning," he called.

"Morning, morning!" whispered the butterfly in the wind.

"You have been out for a long time!"

"I'm heading home," Hugs said. "But first, could you give me a kiss?"

"A kiss from me?" The butterfly dipped his wings.

"Yes, please, a kiss right here." Hugs pointed to his mouth.

So the butterfly settled gently on
his mouth and gave him a kiss.
Hugs closed his eyes again and
smiled. Oh, so fine, a butterfly's kiss!
He'd never felt anything like it before.
It tickled a bit of course, but it
was wonderful.
Hugs thanked the butterfly with
all his heart and hurried on home.

His mother and father and sisters were all waiting
for him.
"Where have you been?" asked Mother. "We were
worried about you."
"Oh, it was such a beautiful morning, I couldn't sleep.
And there was something I had to find out."
"Now my little one, what was so important?" Mother
nuzzled Hugs and gave him a big kiss.

"That's it!" Hugs said. "Now I know:
A kiss from a duck is refreshing.
A kiss from a horse is warm,
A kiss from a pig is tender,
A kiss from a rabbit is soft,
A kiss from a butterfly is wonderful…
But the best kiss of all is the kiss I get from you!"